Text copyright © 1999 by Ana Maria Machado
Illustrations first published in *Quelle Fête!*, copyright © 2005
by Vents d'ailleurs / Ici & ailleurs
English translation copyright © 2013 by Elisa Amado
Published in Canada and the USA in 2013 by Groundwood Books

Groundwood Books / House of Anansi Press
110 Spadina Avenue, Suite 801, Toronto, Ontario M5V 2K4
or c/o Publishers Group West
1700 Fourth Street, Berkeley, CA 94710

We acknowledge for their financial support of our publishing program the
Government of Canada through the Canada Book Fund (CBF).

Library and Archives Canada Cataloguing in Publication
Machado, Ana Maria
What a party! / written by Ana Maria Machado ;
illustrated by Hélène Moreau ; translated by Elisa Amado.
Translation of: Mas que festa!
ISBN 978-1-55498-168-7
I. Moreau, Hélène II. Amado, Elisa III. Title.
PZ7.M1795Wh 2013   j869.3'42   C2012-905124-1

The illustrations were done in acrylics and oil pastel.
Design by Michael Solomon
Printed and bound in Malaysia

What a Party!

Ana Maria Machado

PICTURES BY
Hélène Moreau

TRANSLATED BY ELISA AMADO

GROUNDWOOD BOOKS   HOUSE OF ANANSI PRESS

TORONTO   BERKELEY

areful, be very careful!

If a few days before your birthday your mother should say, "I think I'm going to bake a cake and buy some juice. Why don't you ask one of your friends to come over to play?" you might do what I did and remember that Jack has a really cool brother.

And then you might say, "Well, could Jack bring someone and maybe some food too?"

And then your mother, feeling a bit distracted, might answer, "Why not? Of course. Invite anyone you'd like."

If that happens, and you don't watch out, you might end up writing an invitation like this one:

Come to my party. It's my BIRTHDAY. Bring along whoever you want and whatever you like to eat.

And if Jack comes with his brother, Larry, maybe they'll bring a soccer ball. And their mother might decide to bake two different kinds of coconut cookies, so that they don't arrive empty-handed.

And if Beto and Antonieta, who own a
cute parrot that they couldn't bear to leave
at home, come too, because Jack mentioned
it to them, then for sure their mother, Juana,
might send along a pineapple, some mangos
and a passion fruit.

And if Fatima, who is Antonieta's best friend, decides to bring her brother, Djamel, maybe they'll have to drag along their dog. And their mother, Mrs. Khelil, might make tajine with olives and pickled lemons just to calm people's hunger pangs.

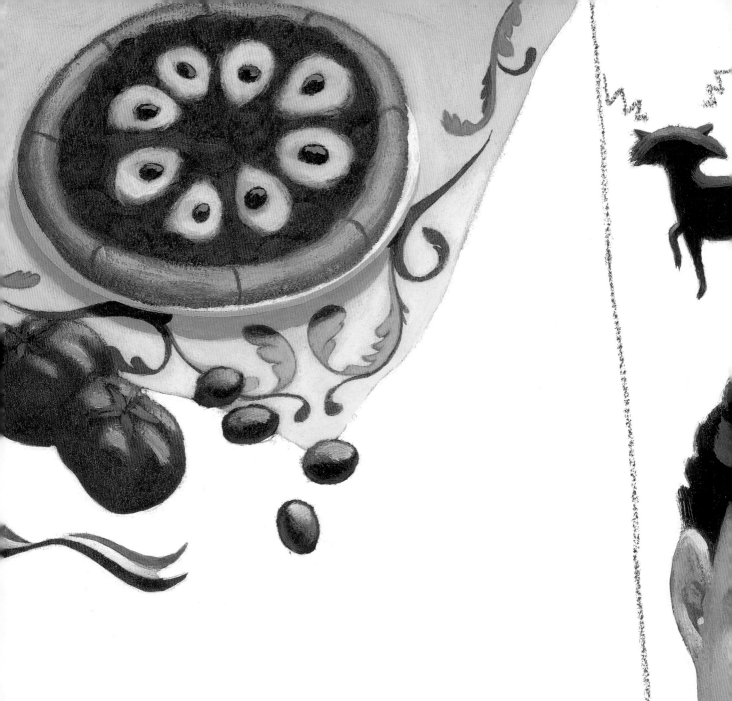

If Tony hears about it and comes with his
cousin, Carlo, they might not bring the cat, but
Tony's mother, Signora Gina, is certain to send
half a dozen large pizzas already cut up and
some gelato for dessert.

And if Hannah shows up with her little brother, Willy, who always tags along, they are pretty sure to want to bring their canary, Tweetie, to meet Antonieta's parrot. And their mother loves to bake Black Forest cake and springerle.

And when Maria, the neighbor, realizes what's up, Manuel and his macaw, Mateus, are sure to arrive loaded down with little pots of flan to go with the cod cakes Maria makes that are so delicious.

Carmen's mother
might not have time to
make paella on such short
notice, but she'll want to
pack some olives.

And Mrs. Tanaka might not let Tamio bring his turtle, but she won't let him leave the house without some of the sushi she's just made for a special treat.

It won't be easy to find room on the table for all this food, even without the couscous, crepes, salad, stuffed snapper, fried sardines, ackee, spring rolls, fried rice and…

Ahmed will have already set up the barbecue to roast a whole lamb, knowing there's time, because even though James and his rap group are always late, they will eventually show up for sure...

...and join in with
the salsa dancers and
the reggae band.

If you aren't careful, you might have
to clear some space for a soccer match or
find the old basketball hoop for a pick-up
game. There will be lots of noise because
people won't be able
to stop talking even
while they're eating
and dancing and...

The whole night could
come and go, and a new
day begin, especially if the
parents drop in and start
having drinks and chatting
instead of going home.

For all these reasons, be careful. Be very careful. If you don't watch out, your birthday party could turn out to be the craziest, wildest, funnest party ever.

Happy birthday!